MAIL ORDER BRIDE

A Bride for Ethan

SUN RIVER BRIDES
BOOK 3

KARLA GRACEY

Dedication

I dedicate this book to my mother, as she was the one who kept urging me to write, and without her enthusiasm I would never written and published my books.

Contents

Chapter One

"You look like you could take on a rattler, a mountain cat and still have enough anger left over to tackle Mrs Wainwright," Cook said as Maggie stormed back into the kitchens at Young's Hotel.

"Don't even get me started Ellen, and I think it might be best if I stay out of the way of our erstwhile housekeeper or I may find myself out on the streets without a character," she said thoughtfully. "I have about had it up to here with idiots today."

"So who was foolish enough to rile you this time?" Maggie sank into a chair by the fire and looked at her friend's earnest face. Ellen never got angry at anybody, but Maggie seemed to have been born furious. It was as if she had been born in the wrong place and at the wrong time. She seemed to want everything that her gender weren't supposed to - like a career and purpose in life. She had no issue with women who longed to be wives and mothers, but something inside her had always been crying out for more. Men were allowed to have both a home and a family, why should bright and capable women be any different?

Many years ago she had felt forced into making a choice, one that had cost her much, though it had set her on a path to the success she had achieved, becoming second in command in the vast kitchens of one of Boston's finest hotels. Though she was sure she had been right to take the risks she had, there was still something missing – and so her annoyance seemed destined to haunt her forever. But knowing something wasn't enough had never been something she could accept and so she was sure there had to be a solution. There had to be a man out there, somewhere, who could accept that she had as much ambition as he?

Her mentor looked at her with compassion.

"So you have placed your advertisement?" she asked. Maggie nodded. "And it didn't go well?"

"I am not a young woman in need of rescuing Ellen, you know that. How dare that little fool treat me in such a way, it isn't some pimply clerk's job to humiliate and belittle me because I am a strong woman prepared to take a stand to create the future I want."

"Oh dear, the poor lad. I presume his ears will be ringing for a week?" her friend gave her a wry smile. Maggie had to grin, Ellen knew her so very well.

"No I kept my temper for a change, but I was tempted. That little brat couldn't have been more than sixteen and he had the cheek to ask me to supper when he saw the advertisement I was placing. The horrible creature assumed I must be desperate!"

"You have to admit Maggie, very few women would take such a step. It is easy to misconstrue such an action."

"Oh stop being so kind. He was in no way being kind and charitable, nor did he actually want to take me to supper. He was being rude and offensive and thought it all a joke."

"Oh Maggie, are you sure this is such a good idea? After all, if the young man at the newspaper thought it all a joke had you not wondered what kind of responses you may be likely to receive? What if the only people who respond are reprobates and bandits?"

"Either would be preferable to that tow-haired little fool at the Matrimonial Times office," she said with a grin. "Of course I have thought about it, long and hard, as you well know. But I am never going to find a man here, and if I apply to an advertisement I have no control over whether he picks me and I have only a few lines to try and find out if he is good and kind. At least this way I am the one choosing, and I am the one who can decide yes or no." Ellen looked at her, skepticism in her eyes but she didn't say any more.

Maggie had been working at Young's since she turned fourteen. She was now twenty- seven and she had watched girls leave and find husbands who were less capable, far more stupid, and occasionally less pretty than her. She was fed up of it always being everyone else's turn and she was never going to find a man while she was tucked away where nobody could ever see her. She loved her work, and had risen to being second in command to Cook, who ruled the kitchens as if they were an extension of her own loving family. But she had deserved to do well and she wanted a family, and though she was self-sufficient she longed for a man to care for her, who she could care for too. So, when she had seen that women were beginning to place their own advertisements in both the Boston Globe now, and in the Matrimonial Times, she knew it was time to take a chance.

The days passed slowly as she waited for the first responses to arrive. She knew that she would only be likely to attract a certain kind of man – few would be strong enough in themselves to welcome a woman so independent that she would take such matters into her own hands. But she was prepared for the oddities that may respond too. She prayed that somewhere out there was a strong man who would be happy to let her be a strong woman – and wouldn't mind that she was a little bit older, a little bit more set in her ways.

* * * * *

Talented Cook, seeks a kind and honest man with a view to matrimony. He should be happy to let her be as she is, and not try and change her. He should enjoy laughing and be well read. To like children and to consider the possibility of a family would be welcomed. The subscriber is happy to make and maintain a loving home and would be happy to take on the responsibility of a child not her own. All Responses to Box 476, Matrimonial Times

Ethan looked at the advertisement his sister had circled in bright red ink. Annie would never be so crude as to tell him to his face that he needed a wife, but she had her ways. It made him chuckle to think of her poring over the newspaper just for him. He was more than happy on his own, and he simply couldn't understand why Annie was so insistent that he was lonely. He had never been happier since they had moved here to the ranch just outside Sun River, Montana. Herding cattle seemed to come naturally to him, and he had to admit he enjoyed the solitude of being away with the herd so much too. It gave him much needed respite from the demands of being part of such a huge family once more.

"Annie, you need to be a little more subtle," he said with a grin as she waddled into the kitchen, her swelling belly and happy face telling a story all their own. "You have to stop trying to get us all to settle down. We'll do it when we're ready."

"I can't seem to stop myself. Myra said I was nesting, that I want everyone around me settled and content, and life as stable as possible around me. It's something pregnant women do apparently. But, I think it is just because you always look so sad. Ethan, you are a wonderful young man and it would be good for you to have a wife. You're nearly thirty after all."

"And that is your criteria for when a man needs a wife? I have a full four years before I turn thirty, so come back and nag at me then. In the mean time, why not find John a wife – he seems to be much more inclined to go in search of female company than I."

"Which is why I don't need to give him a nudge you great galoot. And because at only eighteen he needs some of his rough edges smoothed off before any poor girl should have to be expected to take him on!"

Ethan shrugged. Maybe she was right. Maybe the fact he was always so tongue tied around girls was because it meant so much more to him than it did to John. His younger brother was one of those people who seemed to have more confidence than they should, but he wasn't arrogant or mean with it. He just knew who he was. Ethan had never felt so certain.

He wondered if it had something to do with being the eldest boy in a family that was almost split into two generations. He and Annie were both so much older than Hannah and John because Mama had sadly lost a number of babies in between them.

The two of them had been forced to grow up early and take responsibilities beyond their years. Everything had changed for them after Papa had died, and Mama had taken ill. Both he and Annie had gone out into the world to do the best they could to support their family while Hannah and John had been left at home to care for Mama, despite their own tender years. It had been tough for them all, but Ethan and Annie had ensured that both of them got to attend school too – a luxury that neither of them had been so lucky to receive.

But consumption had finally taken its toll, and the family had fragmented; each going their own way. Ethan had started out working in Boston as Annie had, but as work for uneducated men became more scarce in the bustling city he had been forced to move further afield, and had taken jobs wherever he could find them. John had become a clerk at the local court house, and Hannah - well she was still so young when Mama had died, and with Ethan in Colorado by then and Annie in service nobody could take her in, and John had been too young. So she had been made a ward of the courts and had been taken against everyone's wishes into the Boston orphanage. But her siblings' continuing financial support had meant she could continue her education and she was as bright as a button.

At least, that had been the way it was right up until Annie had gotten married to Mack. The sentimental soul had tracked them all down, had paid for them to come as a surprise for Annie. He had even managed to get the court to award Hannah's guardianship to them now they were married and such pillars of their local community. Everyone had been delighted to be back together once more, but the close proximity of so many people living together after years of solitude could be tough at times too.

Ethan had been impressed by his brother in law's generous and thoughtful gesture when the telegram had finally caught up with him in

Alabama, where he had been working as part of a logging crew. Annie had been the only one of his siblings who had written to him religiously as he had made his way across the country, trying all manner of different jobs in his attempt to find a home and a career he could love. He wouldn't have missed her wedding for anything – and then when Mack had offered them all work and a home together once more he had almost wept. But it seemed that his years of solitary wanderings had made it tough to spend so much time around others and so his work on the land gave him the respite he needed.

Annie kissed him on the forehead and bustled outside. He picked up the newspaper again and re-read the words highlighted so clearly. This woman didn't sound like any woman he had ever known. No, that wasn't true. This woman sounded exactly like the one woman who had captured his heart and held it tightly in her grasp ever since. But, it couldn't be. She had been so adamant that a husband and children were not things she wished to appear in her future. But he knew things could change, people changed. He knew he had. But that made it even more unlikely it could be her. He couldn't really be so lucky to find that she was still available, and more to the point looking for a husband, could he? But did he truly wish to see her again after the way she had so ruthlessly trampled over his heart?

But even if it wasn't her, it was someone like her and there could only be a small amount of women that feisty, that determined and that independent in the world. Maybe he might get lucky, and by applying he just may find himself someone capable of wrenching his heart away from the phantom grasp of his childhood sweetheart after all this time. Annie was right; he did need to settle down. He longed to be a part of a loving relationship just like the one she shared with Mack – but he wouldn't settle for second best and most women were just too darn insipid these days. He needed a woman not scared to speak her mind, a woman that took risks and fought for what she believed in. The woman in this advertisement sounded like she just might fit the criteria. But would she be able to live up to his memories, his dreams? There was surely only one way to find out.

Chapter Two

Maggie pushed the stray strands of hair back from her face and then returned her attention to the large mass of dough she was kneading. She loved baking. Just the idea of it fascinated her. How the simple ingredients of flour, water and starter could create something so fluffy and delicious and good never failed to astound her. As she felt the dough become silky under her hands she popped it carefully into a bowl and put it by the fire to prove gently, while she took up the next batch. Kneading was soothing. It helped her to get rid of the anger, the frustrations that seemed to bubble up within her all the time.

"Maggie, do you think you would be able to take responsibility for the kitchens for a couple of weeks?" Mrs Wainwright was suddenly standing by her side. The stern housekeeper had a tendency of moving so silently you didn't even notice she was there until it was too late, and it was more than a little disconcerting.

"Of course, is Cook all right?" she asked concerned. Ellen had been looking a little tired recently, and Maggie knew she was worried about her sister who lived on the family farm a little way upstate.

"Yes, but her sister has sadly passed away and Cook needs to arrange and attend the funeral. I have assured her that the kitchen will be in safe hands, but you know how she worries." Maggie was stunned. Mrs Wainwright had always appeared to be cold as ice, with no compassion for a soul. Yet here she was, clearly concerned for Cook. But, she supposed that the two women had worked together, here at Young's, for over twenty years and had both reached the pinnacles of their domain - it was to be expected that they should have some kind of relationship – even if it was never on show to the staff around them. Ellen could have confided in her of such a thing, especially when she thought of the amount of times she had berated the women who now looked so genuinely concerned. She had to admit, she felt a little ashamed of herself for doing so now.

"Tell her to take as long as she needs Ma'am, I can take care of everything here. I shall arrange something from the staff here in the kitchen for her, to let her know we are thinking of her."

"That would be kind. The hotel will, of course, send flowers on behalf of all the staff but I know she would be touched by something a little more personal from you all." Maggie was sure she saw the flicker of a tear in the steely grey eyes, but Mrs Wainwright had turned and left long before she could confirm it. Who would ever have thought that the old dragon had any feelings at all? But, that wasn't what was important now. She had to catch Cook before she left.

She ran up the back stairs to the senior staff's bedrooms and without knocking she barged into Cook's. She looked up, startled. Her eyes were red rimmed, and puffy. "Oh Ellen I am so very sorry for your loss," she blurted as she rushed forward to hug the woman who had been like a mother to her over the years. "You've been so wonderful listening to me moan and complain about the trivial troubles in my life, and barely said a word about how serious things were for poor Patricia."

"So Millie spoke with you then?"

"Mille? Mrs Wainwright is a Millie?" Maggie asked incredulously. "I had her down as something altogether more fearsome – maybe Ermentrude or Earnestine!" Ellen gave her a tight little smile.

"You are ever so naughty, even now. You need to try and curb that just a mite love," she warned.

"I doubt I'll change much now Ellen. But, other than taking care of things here, is there anything else I can do for you?"

"No, you just keep things ticking here. I'll be back in no time. There isn't much to sort out. Patricia wasn't a wealthy woman. Like me she lost her husband young, but she has a daughter and she will need my support."

"Take however long you need Ellen, don't rush back. We'll be more than all right."

"I know sweetheart. You're a good girl." Maggie gave her another quick squeeze, and turned to go.

"I've had some replies," she said suddenly. Ellen looked up at her and smiled.

"Now that is wonderful news. You know, I've always thought it such a shame you let that young man of yours get away when you first came here. He always struck me as the sort that would have been more than happy for you to have your career too."

"I know, but I didn't see that until it was too late and I had sent him packing. The world doesn't make many like him sadly. But let's hope that someone just like him will be hiding in the pile of letters I have to look through and I will be able to make amends after all." Ellen stood up and moved towards her. Patting her affectionately on the cheek she gazed steadily into Maggie's eyes.

"Don't be so stubborn this time." Maggie laughed wryly.

"That is like asking a light not to shine, or the sea to not be salt!"

"I know, but you can do it. Be gentle on him and yourself. Good luck and write to me about it all."

"I shall. Safe journey. Now I really must get back to the bread or there will be no loaves for lunch."

She ran back downstairs, wiping furiously at the tears pouring down her cheeks. Poor Ellen, she was being as stoic and brave as always – and dispensing good advice too. Maggie wasn't sure why she had confided in her, but was glad she had. Ellen was the only person who had known about her young man all those years ago – and that she had pushed him away because she had been so set on having a career and had believed that a husband would only hold her back. She had regretted it ever since, but he had disappeared and she was left wondering what might have been.

The pile of letters still sat on the kitchen table. She had been using the bread making as a distraction, too nervous to even look at a single one. But with Ellen's words of encouragement she sat down and began to sort them quickly. She was stunned to see that there were over thirty of them. Each had a neatly printed envelope and the return address of the Matrimonial Times. People had actually responded, and in such numbers. She hadn't expected there to be so many men interested in her. She had worded her advertisement so clearly – to make certain they knew she wasn't some simpering little thing and would not be an easy conquest.

She ripped open the first one and scanned the first few lines. The man sounded like a complete idiot. He clearly hadn't read her words at all, had probably just responded to every woman he could. She put it down and opened the next one. He wasn't any more suitable either. She opened and scanned, and threw each letter down getting more and more frustrated. Why had not one of them read her advertisement properly. Each and every one of them was only concerned with what she could do for him, and each and every one seemed to just want a woman to cook and clean and maybe have his babies. Well, that wasn't for her, at least it wasn't the only thing she wanted from her life.

She wanted to be married and she wanted a family, but she did not want it to be her only focus in life. She was talented and clever and she needed more of a challenge than that. She had to hold fast to the belief that there was someone for her, and not allow herself to just throw the remaining letters in the fire. It would be so easy to get dismayed, to believe that every letter would be the same, but she had to be strong. She knew that this would be like looking for a needle in a haystack when she had placed the advertisement. For once she had to be patient. She would save them until later, would read them in privacy in her room. Maybe, just maybe there would be one decent man in this sorry collection?

Her day dragged, and her mood did not improve. She was worried about Ellen and frustrated at life and the caliber of the possible marriage pool open to her. But once she was sitting quietly in her room after supper she took a deep breath and began to open the remaining letters. She knew not to have her hopes too high, but it seemed that even her low expectations had been too much - until she came across a letter written in a sloping script that was strangely familiar.

Dear Talented Cook,

I dare say you have had many replies to your rather unusual and very pertinent advertisement. But I pray that I will be the man you respond to. Your words reminded me of a woman I once knew and she was a real firecracker. I suspect that you may be just as feisty and if so, that would be a wonderful thing.

I do not long for a peaceful and doting wife. I would much rather one with her own ideas and opinions, and a desire to be whoever she wishes to be. If that is to be the mother of my children that would be wonderful, but if she would prefer to have a career of her own I would support her in her every endeavor.

I am a cowboy. I have been a logger, a stevedore, a trapper, a miner, and even tried panning for gold at one time. But my life here in Montana seems to suit me best. I currently share a home with my married sister and her husband. My younger brother and sister live here too. We have been separated for many years, and I would very much like to stay with them, for a time at least. We have missed out on so much in one another's lives.

The ranch I work on belongs to my brother in law, but with the new homesteading opportunities here my brother and I may be able to claim further lands nearby -and so, between us, we could own much of the valley and build quite the enterprise.

Strong women are much needed here in Montana, and those with good hearts and valuable skills are thought much of. I would be honored should you choose to correspond with me, to see if

we might suit. I look forward to finding out more about you.
   Yours most humbly
   Ethan Cahill

Maggie's heart leapt at the sight of the name, so neatly written at the page's end. How could this be? How could kind, loving Ethan not be married and settled? And who was the mysterious firecracker he remembered so fondly? A shot of jealousy surged through her. But then she stopped and looked at his words once more. What if the firecracker was her? Could it be that he still harbored feelings for her? Surely that would be too good to be true? He had once been her very reason for being, but she had never wanted the life of a wife and mother that seemed to be the only path open to her should she remain with him. But, she remembered his gentle eyes and loving ways every day, and her memories of his strong, hard body and tantalizing kisses could still have her feeling flustered even after all these years.

But would he respond once he knew it was her? And if she didn't admit to her identity in her responses, how would she ever be able to explain why she hadn't been honest from the start? But she longed to find out about his adventures, to know how he was. She had to know if he truly was happy, that she hadn't hurt him so badly that he had been lonely ever since she had left him. She jumped up to get paper and pen from her chest, and began to write. The words flowed effortlessly, right up until she reached the point where she had to sign her name. She paused, chewing anxiously on the tip of her pen, still unsure whether to tell him the truth now or later.

Chapter Three

A pounding of hooves on the trail behind him alerted Ethan that he had company. He turned to see his brother's stricken face as he reined his horse in abruptly. "Ethan you've gotta come home," he said. "It's Annie."

"Annie? But everything was coming along fine when I left. She seemed positively glowing." He could feel the anxiety in him grow; they had only been together such a short time. He couldn't bear the thought of losing any of his siblings again.

"No, she's well. It's just the baby, it's coming!" John said excitedly. "She said she'd hang on as long as she could. She wants us all to be there." Ethan could tell by the look on his young face that John was not so happy about this idea.

"Never upset a pregnant woman John, if that is what she wants, then that is what we must do. The herd will be fine here for a few hours I guess. Come on, I'll race you back!" John grinned at him, and they both kicked their mounts to a gallop. John's new gelding was fast, but he was temperamental. Ethan had chosen a sturdy beast, bred by Penelope's new husband. Mack's sister now lived just across the valley from their ranch and Callum Walters, her besotted new husband, was renowned throughout Montana - up as far as Washington in the West and even down in Texas to the south for the quality of his horses. They were ideal for ranching. They could go all day, but they also had a turn of speed that could best any but the finest race horses.

When they returned to the comfortable clapboard ranch house the two men found it in uproar. Penelope had arrived, and she and Hannah were bustling between the main bedroom and the kitchen with hot water and plenty of linens. Mack looked almost distraught as he paced up and down on the porch, while Callum was puffing away on his pipe even though it was still unlit. "How is she?"

"Hannah said she was doing fine, but you hear such stories," Mack said distractedly. Callum's face blanched. He had yet to go through the birth of his first child, but it would not be long as Penelope wasn't too far behind her sister in law. But everybody knew of the dangers women faced in childbirth. It was a wonder they ever let a man near them.

"She is fine. Everything is going well," Penelope said firmly as she waddled outside to give them an update. "I think you will have a strapping son Mack, she's coming along so fast so long as none of you buy us troubles with your worrying!"

"It's being out here and knowing nothing," Mack said. Ethan could hear the frustration in his voice. He had to admit, he wondered why Annie had ordered him back from his work. It wasn't as if he could do a thing other than just sit and wait. "Why can't I come in and see her?"

"Because it isn't right. It's woman's work to do without men under our feet."

"Well you know what tradition means to me Penny. I don't give a fig for it. I'm going up to see my wife." Without waiting for her to react he stormed inside and ran up the steep stairs two at a time, Penelope following as fast as she could.

"Stop, you can't. It isn't right," she remonstrated with him as Ethan and John followed them up. Mack paid her no heed, and stormed into the bedroom. They heard a brief shriek, and then a deep murmuring.

"Penelope, I don't think he's going to listen," Ethan said to her as he laid a gentling hand on her arm. "You need to be calm too, you don't want your little one to come early now do you?"

"Men!" she exclaimed and shook her head in frustration.

"Sorry," Ethan said with a grin. Finally she smiled back at him. "We have seen much worse, it won't shock us one bit."

"I know, you boys are out with calves and foals – in all weathers. But it just feels wrong."

"Come on, let's all go in. If Annie wants us all gone, I will personally drag Mack out of there for you."

Annie was propped up in the bed, sweat pouring down her flushed cheeks. Her legs were spread wide, but covered with a sheet that looked sodden with her sweat. "New sheets for you my love," Penelope said as she began to quickly strip the bed, hardly needing to move Annie at all.

"Thank you." Annie gasped as another contraction rocked through her. "I think I need to start pushing now."

"Do you want me to banish them all?" Ethan asked nodding towards John and Mack who were holding a hand on either side of his sister.

"No, I'm glad you are all here. It feels right to have my entire family here."

Mack sat on the bed, and pulled his wife against his body. "You scream and holler all you want," he assured her as she rested into his solidity. "But, if you need to squeeze hard on a hand, I'd be glad if you made it John's!" he joked. Everyone laughed, but another contraction came swift and fast, and so the moment of levity soon passed.

Ethan was impressed as he watched Hannah and Penelope guide Annie through her ordeal. It was clearly painful, but thankfully it was swift. Almost as soon as Hannah told her sister to begin pushing they could see the head of the baby and with just a few good pushes he was out and hollering up a storm. Ethan was moved more than he would ever have imagined as he watched his youngest sister carefully swaddle the child and take it to its mother.

"Have you done that before?" he asked her quietly as she began to tidy away all the soiled linens.

"There were always women nearby having babies Ethan, it wasn't as if you can stand by and do nothing." He knew of many people who had lived in the tenements in which they had grown up who would have done nothing to help a single soul. "But, I also helped out at the orphanage. Often young girls would come to us, to have their child in safety and then leave the babe with us."

"I'm so sorry we had to leave you there Hannah."

"I don't mind. I was happy there, in my own way. I learnt a lot of useful things, and you and Annie made sure I could still go to school. I'd like to become a midwife. I think it would be wonderful to be able to help women as they go through this."

"You'd be wonderful at it, if this was an example of your skills. You kept Annie calm as anything," he said admiringly.

"Oh, Ethan," Annie said weakly from the bed, a look of absolute infatuation in her eyes as she gazed down at her beautiful new son, "there was a letter for you yesterday. I put it on the mantle, behind the pewter candlestick for you."

"Only you would remember a thing like that, at a time like this," he said giving her a smile. "Congratulations to you both," he added as he shook Mack's hand and moved forward to kiss Annie and the new baby on the forehead.

"Would you mind if we call him Henry?" Annie asked Mack cautiously.

"Not at all, but why Henry?"

"Because Henry was Papa's name," Ethan said, spying a tear in his sister's eye. John and Hannah all nodded, and he pulled them to him. "He'd be proud as punch Annie."

He ushered his siblings from the room, and found Callum waiting awkwardly on the stairwell. "You could have come in, none of us would have minded," Ethan said as he slapped the quiet man on the shoulder affectionately.

"It was a moment for family, it wouldn't have been right."

"You are family Callum." The shy man blushed beet red at the compliment and beamed at Ethan. "You are the proud uncle of a new baby boy called Henry, go on in and meet him."

He went downstairs and walked into the parlor, where the letter Annie had spoken of sat awaiting him. "John, could you maybe ride over and tell Myra and Carlton the good news? He asked as he sank down into the comfortable wing chair by the fire.

"Anything to get out of here!" his younger brother said, poking his head around the door. "Can I go up and check on the cattle once I'm done? It would be nice not to have to come back for a day or so while everyone goes silly over the baby."

"That is your nephew John, but yes. I'd be glad of a day or two back here and I don't think Mack will be leaving Annie for a while yet so somebody needs to be up there. Be careful, and any trouble you come right back here, d'you understand?" John nodded. They had never left him alone with the herd, but he was more than capable. He could just be a little too impetuous at times. But he could understand why an eighteen year old boy didn't want to be in a house with a new baby.

Ethan picked up the ivory handled letter knife from the table beside him and slit through the cream envelope. It had come from Boston, and he could only hope that meant he had received an answer from the mysterious advertiser. Other than Maggie, he had never really found women that distracting, but in recent weeks he had found himself continually wondering what the intriguing woman who had placed that advertisement might be doing, who was she, and why was she in search of a man?

> "*Dear Mr Cahill,*
>
> *I was delighted to receive your response to my advertisement. You would not believe how many of the men who did respond were clearly complete imbeciles! To find at least one who knew how to construct a sentence, and who had clearly read my advertisement properly was most refreshing. I have been told by*

many that I am too forthright, and just a little bit too aggressive. But I am a redhead, and the passion inside just seems to leak out at times. I know what I want, and I have a tendency to not stop until I have whatever my heart desires.

I am a cook in one of the finest hotels in the city. I cannot imagine my life without my work. I enjoy it, and get great satisfaction from it. I hope that honesty does not affront you in any way – but I do feel it best to let you know exactly the kind of woman I am. However, I do want a family and a husband and so I advertised for just that. I won't sit and wait for a man to come to me!

Your past love, is she someone you are still in contact with? Do you still harbor feelings for her? I do not wish to be rude, but I will not diminish myself in that way. I am a woman in my own right, and deserve to be loved for the person I am – not because I may remind you of somebody you once knew.

I am glad for you that your family has found one another again. I would not wish to take you from that life now you have it. But this may leave us in a little bit of a quandary. I have my position here in Boston, which I have no desire to leave. You seem to be settling happily in Montana. So, do you expect me to come to you, or would you be prepared – maybe in time as I can entirely appreciate your need to be amongst family now – to come here to Boston? If we cannot settle this one fundamental issue, then maybe it might be best if we did not correspond further?

Yours Sincerely

Miss Smith

The wording was as forthright as her advertisement, and it made Ethan chuckle – until he reached the part where she was already suggesting that they stop their correspondence before it had even begun. A pang of anger grabbed his heart as he realized that she was pushing him away. But why? What offense could she possibly have taken from his letter? But, then he began to look back over her letter. She gave him no obvious clues as to where she was working, did not give her name, and bristled at the possibility he may be trying to replace his lost love with her.

He knew that there could be a thousand Miss Smith's in America – but two that had red hair and worked in a fine hotel in Boston as a cook? That seemed to be too much of a coincidence. This was his Maggie, he was sure of it. She must have realized who he was immediately and in her blunt, yet oddly evasive way she was telling him that she did not want him. He felt his heart sink, and knew the pain of losing her all over again.

But she wanted a husband. And she longed for a family. She had told him that she never wanted those things, though he had always been sure that she was lying. He had tried back them to find a way to convince her to let him prove he was the kind of man who would let her be, and would gladly help with keeping the house and bringing up the children so she could continue to do so. But it had not been enough for her then, and clearly it was not now.

He took the letter upstairs to Annie. She and Maggie had been close once, and he was sure that she would know if Maggie was pushing him away because she had never loved him, or if it was something deep within her that made her distrustful of any man. He had always been so sure that she loved him, yet her behavior then and now surely told him otherwise – but he didn't believe it, not even in black and white on the page.

"I know you should be resting, and I don't want to interrupt the time you have with Mack and young Henry, but I need you." The little family were huddled together on the bed, the proud parents beaming down at the tiny, perfect little creature they had brought into the world.

"Mack, could you take Henry and put him down for a nap?" Annie said and patted on the bed beside her, indicating that Ethan should sit. Mack took Henry from her arms, and kissed her on the forehead.

"Have a sleep yourself when you are done, I'll bring him in when he gets cranky for his supper!" Annie smoothed the downy hair on her son's head, and smiled at them both.

"Thank you," she said and then waited as they left the room.

"What is it?" Ethan gave her the letter. She read it, and sighed heavily. "You answered the advertisement then?"

"I did. She sounded so like Maggie and I hoped that maybe there were two of them in the world and I might be lucky enough to keep hold of one this time," he admitted sadly.

"Oh, Ethan you old romantic! I always knew you had never really gotten over her."

"It is her isn't it?" he asked, half of him praying she would agree with him that it was, the other hoping it simply couldn't be.

"I think so. I doubt they made another one quite like her. But Ethan, do not be downhearted. She has given you enough clues to know it is her. I think she is praying that you will forgive her, will go to her."

"Really?" he asked incredulously. "I just see her pushing me away again."

"She knew it was you. She also knew just how much she hurt you, and herself when you were younger. She would feel that she had no right to expect you to just forgive her, or to even ask for that forgiveness. Look, here," she pointed at the letter. "Weren't those exactly the words you said to her when she went to work at Young's?" He looked again. Annie was right, they were. The exact terms. He had called her forthright, aggressive, blunt and rude in that final, horrible encounter.

"Annie, what if it is someone else and they just aren't interested?"

"It isn't. It simply couldn't be. It is too like her in every way. She loved you, yet pushed you away. She is doing it again because somewhere inside she thinks she doesn't deserve you – she never did."

"But that is such nonsense."

"No, Maggie had a tough life too. But she was determined to never let anyone have the power to ruin her life again. That is what you have to find out. Who was it, and why she has never let herself trust a soul since."

"So you think I should go to her, and what? Just ask her? She won't tell me. She wouldn't say a word then, why should she now?"

"No, I don't think you should go to her at all. I think we should ask Peter, Myra's Uncle to see what he can find out. I think you should continue to write to her. Be your usual sunny and positive self. Keep telling her that it is who she is that matters most, and her happiness is all you desire. Try not to let on that you know who she is, flirt a little – woo her!"

"But…" he tailed off. She was right. Maggie would be spooked if he ran to Boston to confront her. It would back her into a corner and out of stubbornness it would ruin everything for them both. More than ever he was sure that she still cared for him – had never stopped loving him and he knew he had always held her in his heart. He just had to let her come to him.

Chapter Four

Maggie was stunned to see a thick envelope sitting in the box she had hired at the postal office to hide her location from Ethan. He had always deserved so much more than she could ever offer him and she would not hurt him again. She took it out and saw his looping script and couldn't stop herself from smiling. He hadn't given up on her! But, she had no clue what he had written inside and he may be furious with her for such a blunt and unpleasant response to his kindly letter. She hurried to the park, and found a quiet spot to sit and read it without prying eyes intruding.

Dear Miss Smith

I trust that this letter will find you well. Thank you for your very honest response to me, and your categorically unambiguous approach to life. I agree, there are potentially some issues we will have to consider at some point, but might it be possible for us to converse a while longer until we know each other well enough to know whether such changes may indeed be required?

I shall never be upset, or put off by a woman who speaks her mind. I have always had the utmost respect for the wisdom and capability of the fairer – but not weaker –sex. How could I not, when I have a strong and capable sister, who has ever been the one I turn to when I am in need of advice? I should also consider the backbone of my younger sibling, Hannah, too who deals with a crisis both calmly and sensibly. They truly are both quite remarkable human beings.

The most exciting news I have is that my older sister, Annie, has just given birth to a fine and healthy boy. They named him Henry for our Papa. He has certainly inherited his lungs, and can yell the whole house down when he so desires. Annie and Mack, her husband, are proud as can be – and secretly so am I. John is a little nonplussed by it all. I think he has enjoyed being the youngest boy – maybe he feels a little usurped. But, he is also only eighteen and I don't remember being particularly enamored of babies myself then. Hannah is over the moon. She is determined to become a midwife, and having seen how calmly and carefully she assisted Annie I do think it could be her calling.

There is a new hotel opening in Great Falls next year. According to the gossip, they are aiming to outdo all of the big establishments in Boston, New York and Chicago. There will be electricity throughout, and each room is to have its own bathroom – though I have no idea how he intends to afford such a thing! But, can you imagine? People will flock to it in their droves, and when people then get to see the beauty of Montana and feel the benefit of the clean air and wonderful scenery, the town will be set as a fashionable tourist destination forever.

Montana truly is blossoming, I shall hardly recognize it soon it will be so debonair! But, as long as they don't take away my mountains, and the glorious waterfalls that are all around us here then I shall be content.

Please do continue our correspondence, I believe there is no issue you have concerns over that cannot be addressed and dealt with, when the time comes.

Yours Hopefully

Ethan Cahill

Maggie was almost in tears as she read his words. As always, he was so kind and thoughtful of her needs, her wants. She did not deserve such a kind and good man, she never had. But, she was also delighted for dear Annie. They had been inseparable as girls, and Annie had long dreamed of having her own family. That they had named him Henry was testament to a good man. She had always wished her own Papa had been more like theirs. But, that was in the past now. She was sure he knew it was her, and though she knew that she should probably end the correspondence now, he had made the choice. He had written back, knowing that she had hurt him once and probably would do so again. If he was prepared to take the risk, then surely she could too?

It wasn't as if he had jumped on a train and rushed to her side, no he had only required that they continue to correspond. What harm could there be in that? He was not professing his love through all eternity, nor even marriage. She did not have to ever meet with him, and could continue to hope that another response would come from someone who would pose less of a threat to her heart. She could have this brief interlude of happiness and pleasure, couldn't she?

She stuffed the letter into her reticule and rushed back to her room in the hotel where she re-read his words. Oh, he was so very clever and sweet and dear. To so carefully give her news of her friend's happiness – and even that there could be a job opening for her should they decide they did suit. He hadn't changed. He could still make her feel that she was the center of his world, and that all problems could be overcome – but she knew that some scars could never heal.

The next few weeks rushed by in a flurry of activity. Boston was hosting a grand exhibition, and the hotel was full to capacity. People were arriving from all over America, and she had met a few interesting people from Europe and even Africa too. Everybody was excited by the future. Progress seemed to be happening at such a rate. Young's was no longer unusual, many hotels now had electricity throughout, but they were still the first and this meant that many of the scientifically minded young men made a pilgrimage to see it firsthand.

Maggie was glad of the distraction. Being so busy gave her no time to regret the chatty and more open reply that she had sent to Ethan, nor to consider that she was being a fool to do so knowing that there could be no future for them. She had never baked so much bread, or so many pastries in all her life, but she found he enjoyed the singular focus on just one aspect this had given her. She began to wonder if she would even wish to continue to work in a hotel. Maybe there was an alternative. She began to dream of being a baker in a tiny town, tucked away in the foothills of the Montana mountains, and it was a good dream.

"Maggie love, thank you for all your help," Ellen said as she bustled past, a large casserole full of rich stew in her arms. "You have always had such a gift with dough of all kinds."

"I am just glad it is all over," she laughed, pulling out the cutlery to lay the table for the staff's supper. Cook plonked the large dish down, and Nat and Matthew arrived with tureens full to the brim with buttered peas and boiled potatoes. "That smells delicious." It looked it too. Her mouth began to salivate as everybody began to collapse tiredly onto their chairs around the vast table. She sank into her own, and accepted a ladle full of the rich beef concoction, and then piled the plate high with the delicious vegetables.

"Did you ever hear anything from your advertisement?" Ellen asked her quietly.

"I did, but nobody was worth considering."

"Your frown tells me something different Maggie. And don't you dare try and tell me you don't want to talk about it. I know you. I virtually raised you. You think you are so tough, that you can deal with everything alone, and you have pushed virtually everyone who has ever cared about you away. But, you need us and you need to talk before you end up lonely and bitter like poor Millie." Maggie looked over at the tiny room that Mrs Wainwright kept as a private parlor. She sat, ramrod straight eating tiny bites of her meal. Ellen was right; Maggie certainly did not ever want to end up alone like that.

"I shall tell you later, when all of this lot are out of our hair," she said, trying to smile and reassure her friend. "Now, I have barely had a chance to speak with you and find out how you are since your return from your sister's. How is your dear niece?"

"Samantha is well thank you. She has a sweetheart, and he has proposed. I told her to wait if she wanted, that she did not need to rush into anything because of her Mama, but I think they would have wed soon enough anyway. He is a nice young man. He reminded me a little of your Ethan. Same eyes, and same drive to make something of himself."

Maggie felt a tear welling in her eye, even at the mention of his name. She choked her feelings down and tried to look happy. She could not bear to have anyone feel pity for her. She had made the choice to be alone, to be without Ethan. She should at the very least try and be content with it. But his unexpected reappearance in her life had changed everything, and for once she was going to ask for help – she had to. She couldn't trust herself to make the right decision, because she had clearly been a fool for too long.

Maggie sat quietly in her room after supper, waiting for the knock she knew would come. Ellen did not let her down. She welcomed her in and they sat side by side on her narrow bed. "Maggie love, what is it? I hoped that finding someone to write to might make you happy."

"Oh Ellen, Ethan replied." Cook looked at her with her eyebrow raised quizzically.

"Ethan, your Ethan?"

"My Ethan. He must have seen the advertisement somehow, and he wrote – and keeps on writing no matter how rude I am to him!"

"But Maggie, why ever would you be rude to the only man you have ever loved? Are you trying to push him away again?" Maggie nodded. "But why? Does he know it is you?"

"I think so, though he has not been so crass as to say so. I don't know why I do it Ellen. I do it with everyone but you. I did it to Ethan, to his sister Annie who was my best friend in the world."

"Who hurt you Maggie? Who went when you didn't want them to?"

"I don't know!" she cried, but she did. She just didn't want to admit it. It had been buried inside so long, and she couldn't bear it if it came to light now, to torment her life once more. Ellen held her tightly, and let her sob. She hadn't ever done so before, she had been too afraid to show anyone that she had a weakness - that she cared about anything or anyone.

"Maggie love, you have to let these things out – they fester and ruin your life otherwise. You are a good girl and you don't deserve to be in this pain." But Maggie knew that she wasn't, she was so terrible that even her Papa hadn't loved her, hadn't wanted her, had abandoned her without a care.

Chapter Five

Maggie hadn't sent a reply. Weeks had gone by and Ethan was close to giving up hope of ever hearing from her. He had been sure that Annie had been right, and so he had been light and breezy in his letter and tried to take the pressure of Maggie as much as he could. She had always taken responsibility for everyone's trials and tribulations. He wished he could ease the burden for her, but he had no clue how to do so, given that he had no clue why she was as she was. He was determined not to lose her this time, and vowed that if he hadn't heard anything by Thursday then he would be on his way to Boston to find her and demand that she give him another chance.

He rode in to Sun River. The day was hot, and he was thirsty and so he stopped in at the Whistling Rock Saloon. It was just a long wooden shack, with a long wooden bar – but it did what was needed. Ethan didn't often drink alone, knew few men that did and certainly he was not a man to drink in the daytime. But his utter frustration at hearing nothing from Maggie, or from Myra's Uncle Peter had him kicking his heels. His instincts told him to take action – but there was nothing he could do. He simply wasn't good at dealing with that.

He walked up to the bar and he ordered a beer and a shot of whiskey. "Slow down young'un," Tom, the bar man said with a wink as he was about to down the shot. Ethan stopped and lowered the glass back to the bar.

"You're younger than me Tom," he said. "And, to be honest I don't really care how slow I take it right now.

"I know. I just like saying it! What's up? You aren't usually the kind to be in here at all, let alone before lunchtime. But I am glad you stopped by, not just for the coins in my cash register – but there is some mail here for you. Nobody from the ranch has been down for a while, I guess you've all gone a bit baby crazy," he teased.

"Annie, Mack and Hannah have definitely," he admitted. "But John, well he's his usual grumpy self. I think the lad may grow on me once he is old enough for me to teach him to ride! Thanks for these." He took the pile of mail from Tom and flicked through it. There were a few bills from their feed supplier, and two letters from Boston. One in Maggie's familiar hand and the other in a small, neat script he did not recognize. He checked the return address and saw it was from Judge Peter Walker. At last, he might find something out that could help him to make sense of this all. Quickly he downed the shot, and then the lukewarm beer and rushed outside. He un-hitched his horse and galloped up into the mountains.

He stopped when he reached a tiny cave. He had found it a few weeks ago whilst out hiking. He didn't get much time to relax and just be alone now, and it was quiet and peaceful, nobody seemed to even know it was there. He loved his family, but the house was always so busy and especially now young Henry was there and making his needs known , having a bolt hole had become ever more important to him. He settled himself on the little ledge outside, and let his horse graze on the long grass all around. He ripped open the letter from the Judge and began to read.

Dear Mr Cahill

I am glad to be of service to you, and hope that you find the following information useful to you. Myra assures me that I can trust you, that you will be discrete. I pray that will be the case as I should not be sharing this information with you without Margaret Smith's permission – even though much of it is available in the public court records.

Initially I came up against a bit of a blank when searching for her - that was until I realized that Miss Smith was not always called that. Once I discovered that she was actually born Marguerite Jeanette Kennedy things began to come a little clearer.

The records in the Boston Court House show that Miss Smith is the only daughter of the shipping magnate Charles Kennedy. However, the record shows that he left his family and set up home with a ballet dancer when she was a child. Miss Smith took her mother's maiden name at this time, as did her Mother. The divorce was kept very quiet, and he left them with only very little to live on. Miss Smith's Mother died some ten years ago, I believe you knew her at this time, so it will not be news to you. But Miss Smith was already working to support the income of her family at that time.

I do hope that this information may be of help. I am afraid I cannot offer anything further.

Yours Faithfully

Peter Walker

The information was not much, in truth. But knowing this made Maggie seem more real to him at last. The secrets he had always sensed, the lies she had often told. He had always known, her nostrils would twitch ever so slightly and her lip would curl just a little whenever she told an untruth. It was just one of the things that he had loved about her. But he knew now that he should never have let her get away with those lies, should have made her tell him the truth from the start rather than play along as if he couldn't tell.

She had never spoken of her Father, not once. But, where they lived in the tenements it wasn't that unusual. Many of his friends didn't even know who their Father was, few cared. Those that did have Fathers often complained of beatings and drunkenness. He knew that he and his family had been lucky. Papa had been a good man, though they had lost him too young. Maggie had just been like everyone else, a child with only one parent. But he did remember that she had always seemed to despise anyone with money. She had been scathing in her attacks of those who took their privilege for granted, and her Papa's defection from her could certainly explain that. Poor Maggie, to lose her Father and be left on the scrap heap of life to survive as she might, it just did not seem fair that she was the one still carrying the burden of guilt and fear for something not her fault.

In moments he was back on horseback, and racing towards the ranch. He would go to Boston now, this very minute. He would find her and demand that she tell him why she was always so determined to push him away. He would tell her that he would never leave her, would never toss her away because he had found something or someone else. He loved her, and he always had. He always would. He was determined that she would not do it to him again, would not leave him and condemn them both to a lonely life apart from one another.

He tore into the house and up the stairs. In his room he pulled at drawers randomly, stuffing things into a bag. He would probably find that he had three pairs of pants and no shirts when he arrived, but he had to be at the station in time to get that train. "Ethan, whatever are you doing?" Annie said as she came into the room to find him throwing garments onto the floor and bed in his haste.

"I'm going to Boston. I have to find her, bring her back and let her know that she has a family – she has always had a family."

"I saw the letter on the table, but you haven't opened the one from her. What if she doesn't want you to find her, to rescue her? If I remember rightly Maggie was not the kind of girl who dreamt of a white Knight racing in on his snow white charger to save the poor damsel in distress!"

"She has no darn choice," he growled. "There is nothing she can say that will change my mind."

"I guessed that, but remember to be careful with her. She can be so prickly, and she will do everything she can to push you away. She certainly managed it with both of us before. I miss her too you know – she was a good friend, but it was just so difficult to keep in touch after you left. She didn't seem to want any reminders of you anymore and so she stopped coming back to see me too." Annie sighed. "Here, take this," she thrust a number of ten dollar bills into his hands. "You will need every penny, and read her letter on your way."

Swiftly he hugged his sister and then was on his way once more. He got to the station in Great Falls with time to purchase his ticket and to find a lad to take his horse back home in exchange for a dollar, and he was just about to do so when he saw something he had never expected to see. A young woman was standing at the very front of the queue, asking for directions. She had the most vivid red hair he had ever seen, and an hourglass figure that he simply longed to take in his arms and hold forever.

"Maggie?" he asked incredulously, barging past the surprised people in the queue between them. She turned to face him and her beautiful face lit up with joy. It was her! He wasn't imagining things – though he had begun to wonder for just a moment.

"Ethan," she sighed as she held out her hands to him. He clasped them desperately, as if he were a drowning man and only she could save him. In a way he supposed he was. She was the love of his life, and he could only pray that she wouldn't let him go this time.

"However did you get here?" he asked foolishly, knowing he should have asked why she was here, if she loved him – anything other than something so utterly foolish. She chuckled, and her beautiful green eyes lit up. Unable to control himself any longer he pulled her to him, and crushed his lips to hers. They were soft and yielding, and he felt her hands creep around his back and caress him tenderly. The electricity that had always sparked between them was still there, and he lost himself in the scent of her, the taste of her, and the soft warmth of her against his tired and lonely body.

"I came on the train," she said with a grin when he finally released her. The people around them looked scandalized, but he didn't care. Maggie was here and, if that kiss was anything to go by, she loved him just as much as he loved her. It spoke of hope and possibility – and he was willing to grab onto as much of that as he could get.

"Yes, I know. Stupid of me. Why are you here? Sorry, that sounds pretty harsh, but Maggie you…" He couldn't bring himself to finish the sentence. He had felt a surge of anger course through his veins, that she could be here and so nonchalant. Didn't she know the torment she had put him through, then and now?

"I came to see Annie and to meet Henry of course. Thank you so much for telling me of her wonderful news in your letter," she said in a matter of fact tone. He felt his heart sink, he had so wanted her to be here because she loved him, and finally knew that she couldn't live without him another day. "Oh you lovely, silly man. I am teasing. I am here to see you. You did know it was me you were writing to didn't you?" He could feel the frustration within him rising, knew his eyes were flashing fire. She was teasing him? After everything else she had done?

"I did, but I could hardly believe it was true. How you can simply stand there and be so flippant I do not know? How much more pain do you intend to put me through? Haven't you been cruel enough?" he burst out, unable to keep it in any longer.

"So, you haven't received my last letter then?"

"It arrived this morning. I was going to read it on the train."

"Read it before we speak again," she said mysteriously. "I hope it will explain why I am here, being nervously flippant because I don't have a clue as to whether you still care for me, or could ever forgive me," she said suddenly looking utterly overwhelmed, and so very vulnerable.

"I have never stopped thinking about you Maggie. I love you. That is why it all hurt so darn much!"

"Shhh! Not here. We do have a lot to talk about, and there is much you should know before you make any such declarations Ethan." Her delicate features looked so stern, so unyielding. But, if she didn't love him, then why would she be here? None of it made any sense to him.

"I shall hire a carriage to take you and your luggage to the ranch. Annie will be delighted to see you. She has missed you too," he said finally, putting a protective hand in the small of her back and picking up her luggage. "Is this everything?" he asked looking at the capacious carpet bag. She nodded.

"I thought women always needed trunks of things – knick knacks, fripperies and the like" he admitted. "But then, you were never like any girl I've ever met." She smiled and allowed him to direct her outside. He took her to where the stage coach that passed through Sun River was waiting and went to assist her inside, but she ignored his supportive hand and boarded without it. He kicked himself for being such a fool. Maggie was still the determined and independent woman she had always been. The fact she had come without warning told him that.

He watched the coach set off, and then went in search of the lad he had paid to take his horse to the stable. He was still standing talking to a friend, eating a tasty looking pie. "You can keep the dollar," he said with a grin, certain that his money was how the boy had afforded his meal. He took the reins and then began to make his way back home where he quickly put Mildred between the shafts of the gig and set off into town to meet the stage coach. Main Street was pretty deserted as he pulled up outside the saloon, and he was glad of it. He opened the envelope and pulled out her letter, his hands shaking a little. He wasn't sure what he wanted to read, or what he didn't – but he hadn't been expecting what he did find.

Dear Ethan,

I am sure that by now you know who I am. You have never been a fool, and I doubt if that would have changed. I have much I would tell you, much to beg your forgiveness for – but yet I still do not know where to start.

Firstly, I must apologize for not being honest about my identity from the start. I was unsure if you would wish to continue to write to me if you knew, and did not wish to risk you cutting me off if you were still angry. Yet, I couldn't bring myself to pretend either and so I sent that cruel and ungenerous response to you in the hope I might make you wish to be the one to cease our correspondence. As soon as I saw your dear script, and your name at the bottom I knew nothing had changed for me, and nor would it ever be likely to do so.

But, I also owe you an explanation for why I pushed you away all those years ago. I remember you asking over, and over again why I was breaking our engagement and no matter what I said you were never happy with my answer. But, eventually I did manage to drive you away – and I have been sorry for that ever since. I was a fool. I didn't deserve you then, and I probably still don't now. But, I don't believe that I could ever have answered you sufficiently then – because I simply did not know myself.

I spoke with my dear friend, Ellen, before I wrote this. You may remember her as Cook, the women who taught me everything and loved me like a daughter. I was so scared of her on my first day at Young's, and you were so very supportive of me. To think how things can change, and in such odd ways! Well, Ellen helped me to understand why I pushed you away – and finally helped me to see that that reason was never my fault.

You know Mama died not long after I met you. She had been frail for much of her life. But, there was a reason for that. Mama wasn't born into the life we all led. She was brought up in a world of silk sheets and servants. So was I. But, when Papa decided he wanted a younger wife, who would be prettier on his arm at his soirees, he left us with nothing. He gave Mama barely enough for us to survive. It was why I was so determined to never be like my Mama. I could not ever consider the idea of being dependant on a man, could not leave myself to be so vulnerable should he ever decide to leave.

I hated myself for loving you, for even considering marriage with you – and yet I couldn't ever say no to you. I knew you would never treat me the way Papa had treated Mama – you are the best and kindest man I have ever known – but he had so damaged me that I could not allow myself to believe that then. I am still not sure I can allow myself to believe it now either.

I have built a life for myself. I need never rely on a man ever. Yet I am as lonely as my Mama ever was and my life just as empty – more so as I do not even have a child to care for and love. But I want that to change. I want to change – though I know it will be more than difficult for me to do so. I cannot ask you to give me the time I will need to learn to trust. I cannot ask you to forgive me for the way I treated you. I cannot even ask you to forgive me for trying to hold onto you once more, even if it was only for this very short while. But, you must know that I do love you. I always have. I am sorry, and I always will be.

Yours, forever

Maggie

"Oh you foolish girl," Ethan said as he brushed away the tears that were streaming over his cheeks. "I can forgive you anything, but I will not let you waste one more minute of the time we can be together." He chuckled as he jumped down from the gig as he saw the coach come into view. He was so glad she had finally learned to trust, and had come looking for him. He wouldn't let her get away from him again. Not this time. She had admitted she loved him, and he was going to make sure that she never forgot that.

Chapter Six

Maggie nibbled on her fingers throughout the entire carriage ride from Great Falls to Sun River. She had no idea what to expect when she arrived. Ethan would have read her letter by then, he would know what she finally knew. She prayed she had not pushed him too far, that he could forgive her for everything she had done. She was well aware that she did not deserve a second chance, and felt he would be utterly entitled to dismiss her and send her straight back to Boston – but she prayed that he would not do so.

The coach was full. A rotund man in a smart suit was taking up almost two seats beside her, wedging her tightly against the door and a wealthy looking woman had her two daughters sat opposite her. The lady sat opposite her looked at her ungloved hands and the calluses on them and gave a disgusted "Tsk," before peremptorily turning away. She gave her daughters a look that did not disguise her distaste. The two girls looked away shyly, not wanting to meet Maggie's gaze. She looked at her hands, they showed clearly that she worked hard for a living, but as far as she was concerned that was nothing to be ashamed of. But, her finger nails would be down to the quick if she didn't stop nibbling at them soon. Hurriedly she replaced her gloves and gazed out of the window.

The scenery was indeed just as lovely as Ethan had described it in his letters. She found herself hoping that she would be able to stay and explore it with him, side by side. She longed to trek up the mountains, to play in the snow at the peaks and to swim in the winding rivers and cool, clear lakes that rolled by outside. She felt a weight begin to lift from her shoulders and her heart the nearer she got to her destination, as if the place had magic that could heal her and make her whole at last. But the nearer she got, the more her nerves began to bubble deep inside her. She tried to distract herself by listening to the birds that sang so lyrically all along the route, and even by looking for patterns in the bright, fluffy clouds in the sky. But nothing could soothe the churning turmoil in her belly.

"Sun River," called the driver, banging hard on the roof. Maggie jumped almost out of her skin. It was too soon. She wasn't ready. She had no clue what to say, or how to deal with any of this. She peered anxiously out of the window and saw Ethan waiting for her as the stage pulled up outside the saloon. He looked so calm, so utterly handsome – as he always did, and she realized she had absolutely no idea of what he was thinking. She sat back and took a deep breath, then grabbed her things and took the first step into what she hoped would be her new life.

"Welcome to Sun River," Ethan said as he took her hand and assisted her to alight from the carriage. In the past she would have been furious at any man who did such a thing, but suddenly it felt natural and right to accept Ethan's assistance. It was a long drop, and there was no block to make it easier, and her full skirt made her clumsy. She stumbled a little, losing her balance. He held her tightly, stopping her from falling, and she thought of all the times he had done so in different ways. He had always been there for her, even though she had done little to deserve it. She gazed up into his handsome face, feeling his wiry and strong body pressed up close to hers and longed to reach up and kiss him. But, she knew she could not, not yet.

"I read it," he said, his voice calm and even.

"And?" she demanded, unable to take much more.

"There is nothing in it that could ever have changed the way I feel about you."

"Ethan, I am so sorry that I didn't let myself trust you. I should always have known that you were nothing like my Father. I should have known that you would never do to me what he did to my Mama. But, I was young and silly, and so very scared. I thought he had gone because I was a bad girl, that he couldn't tolerate my bad behavior any longer. It took me such a long time to learn that relationships fail, because people let them. He didn't want us, it was nothing either Mama or I had done.

"When he left, things did not change much - at first. We stayed in the house, and he had so often been away a lot anyway. Mama still acted as his hostess, and he would belittle her and humiliate her in front of everyone as he always had. They all knew he had left us – but they were all such hypocrites. They would gladly come to our home and accept my Mama's hospitality, and laugh at her behind her back. It was all so amusing to them. I think that was when I began to distrust anyone. How could I trust people who could be so cruel to a woman in so much pain?"

"That must have been hard to bear for her, and difficult to understand for you. You were so very young," he said gently. His eyes were so soft, so full of love for her. She had expected pity, but there was nothing but admiration for her written on his face.

"But, then when he decided he wanted to marry Brigitte, well he wanted the house too. He wanted his life to carry on as it always had, and so we were now surplus to his needs. He found us the apartment across from yours, and left us there. I don't think I even realized that it was my new home – not until much later. Mama would say he loved me, would come and see me – but he never did. And, so I stopped looking for him. I stopped looking for his love."

"But by doing so, you stopped allowing anyone else to love you too?" She nodded. She should have known he would understand. Ethan had always been so much more sensitive to others needs than any man she had ever known, more so than many women too.

"I am so glad you understand. I didn't know how to do anything else but feel that way," she sighed, the final wave of tension leaving her body finally. "Now, what is there a girl can do to earn her keep in Sun River?" she said, trying to ease the mood. She began looking around her. Ethan chuckled.

"There isn't much, but we are growing all the time," he said tipping his Stetson back from his forehead and escorting her, tucking her arm in his as they took a walk down the tiny main street.

"I see the saloon, and a hardware store. Is there a grocery store?"

"Nope, that is inside the General Store. It's getting harder for poor Will though, he's not ever got anything the women want these days. He much preferred it when he was only supplying men – they just wanted canned beans, and flour!"

"Do you think there are enough people to want a small bakery?" she asked curiously.

"More than enough, especially if you sold some of the more 'high falutin' stuff' I think it was Will called it!"

"Where should I have my bakery," she asked him, feeling dreamy. He hadn't even proposed, but she was sure he would – and well, if he didn't then she sure would.

"I think right here," he said as they walked up towards a site with a large wooden frame laid out on the ground. "This will be the church, we'll be building it over the next few weeks. We are all chipping in what time we can. A bakery right next door would mean everyone will know where to find you."

"That is a very wise idea," she said with a smile. "Then I shall have to find out how to go about buying this plot of land and building me a little shop."

"You want to stay?" he asked, she could hear the tension in his voice.

"If you want me to?" she said simply.

"I do," he admitted.

"We may have to wait a bit to say that," she teased. "No church!"

"Then we'd better get it built quick, so we can sort that out!"

"Ethan, will you marry me?"

"You never needed to ask that Maggie. You've held my heart since I was just seventeen years old. I've never considered giving it to anybody else." He pulled her against him and held her tightly, she melted into him and finally he felt as if his life was exactly the way it should be.

Epilogue

"Do you Ethan Cahill, take Marguerite Jeanette Smith to be your wife; to have and to hold, for richer and for poorer as long as you both shall live?" the Minister asked him. He looked at his radiant bride and laughed. So many of the vows they were making today did not feel right. He wished they could have written their own, but he dutifully made his response.

"I do," he said and squeezed her hand tightly.

"And do you Marguerite Jeanette Smith take Ethan Cahill to be your husband; to have and to hold, honor and obey as long as you both shall live?"

"I do," she said as she winked at him.

"Then I pronounce you man and wife, you may kiss your bride!"

Ethan bent his lips to his wife's, and kissed them tenderly. They turned and began a slow walk to the end of the church. "I promise to love you even when you are stubborn, to care for you even when you push me away, to always be there for you even when you expect me to leave," he whispered into her ear. She turned and smiled at him.

"And I promise to talk to you when I am troubled, to trust you to love me come what may, to know you love me just the way I am and always will."

"I know it is unlikely, but I wouldn't object to the honor and obey bit too!" he joked. She swatted at him playfully.

"I'm sure you won't hold your breath until I do though."

A crowd clustered around them, and Ethan felt as if his heart might burst. Maggie looked so very beautiful, her long auburn hair trailing down her back. Her green eyes were alight with mischief and happiness, and he wondered what life with her would bring. He knew it would be an adventure. He accepted the warm congratulations of his family, and was glad to see them hugging Maggie just as tightly. Annie had tears in her eyes, as she pulled her old friend to her.

"You take care of him for us," she said, wiping a tear from her cheek.

"I shall, but surely we will be staying at the ranch with you?" she said. Annie gasped, and Ethan looked at her, a stern look on his features. But he couldn't keep angry with her for long.

"Well, I guess I'd better show you your wedding gift then, as Annie has so wonderfully let the cat out of the bag," he said, picking up his wife and cradling her in his arms – despite the howls of protest, and flailing limbs.

"I am not this kind of woman," she told him. "If you'd wanted such a woman you should have found a meek and docile little thing. Now put me down!"

"Nope," he said glad to have her in his arms. "Now calm down little kitten, before you scratch my eyes out and make me no use to man nor beast!" Unwillingly she stopped her twitching and lay calmly in his arms, but the pout on her lips was just too inviting and so he bent his head and kissed her soundly.

He carried her along the street, past her brand new bakery and to a neat, clapboard house. He kept walking, and then turned onto a small trackway, barely big enough for a cart to travel along. "I must be heavy, you can't carry me all the way up the mountain," Maggie said as the path began to climb.

"Oh I think you'll find I can," he said in a low growl.

"I know you are strong, but you don't need to prove anything to me."

"Just be patient, and be quiet," he said as he shifted her weight a little in his arms.

"I'm too heavy," she said impatiently.

"No you aren't. Just stop wriggling!"

Maggie didn't say another word. Ethan had to admit that he was beginning to regret his gallant gesture, as his arms and back began to ache. But as they turned the bend it was worth every moment of agony. "Oh Ethan," she breathed. "Is this our home?"

"Yes my love, John and I have been busy don't you think?"

"I do. It's beautiful."

"And now, I shall carry my bride over the threshold and we shall have a happy life here, together at last. And, you'll notice that we are far enough away from town for us to live however we please – without nosy neighbors to tell us we are wrong."

"Oh Ethan, you truly are the most wonderful man alive," Maggie said as she cupped his face in her palms and kissed him soundly. He stomped up onto the wide porch and kicked open the door.

"I think we are going to be very happy here," he said as they went inside. "But I am truly sorry – I can't manage to carry you upstairs!" he joked as he dropped her unceremoniously into a plush armchair. She giggled.

"I knew you were just being stubborn. I love you Ethan Cahill."

"And I love you, Mrs Cahill – the most stubborn person I have ever known.

The End

Thank you for reading and supporting my book and I hope you enjoyed it.

Please will you do me a favor and leave a review so I'll know whether you liked it or not, it would be very much appreciated, thank you.

Other books by Karla

SUN RIVER BRIDES SERIES

A bride for Carlton #1
A bride for Mackenzie #2
A bride for Ethan #3
A bride for Thomas #4
A bride for Mathew #5

About Karla Gracey

Karla Gracey was born with a very creative imagination and a love for creating stories that will inspire and warm people's hearts. She has always been attracted to historical romance including mail order bride stories with strong willed women. Her characters are easy to relate to and you feel as if you know them personally. Whether you enjoy action, adventure, romance, mystery, suspense or drama- she makes sure there is something for everyone in her historical romance stories!